Captive to Evil

Captive to Evil

JUDE WATSON

SCHOLASTIC INC.

New York Toronto London Auckland Sydney

No part of this publication may be reproduced in whole or in part, or stored in a retrieval system, or transmitted in any form or by any means, electronic, mechanical, photocopying, recording, or otherwise, without written permission of the publisher. For information regarding permission, write to Scholastic Inc., Attention: Permissions Department, 555 Broadway, New York, NY 10012.

Cover art by Maren

ISBN 0-590-18900-X

TM & ® & © 1998 by Lucasfilm Ltd.
All rights reserved. Used under authorization. Published by Scholastic Inc.
SCHOLASTIC and associated logos are trademarks and/or registered trademarks of Scholastic Inc.

12 11 10 9 8 7 6 5 4 3 2 1   8 9/9 0 1 2 3/0

Printed in the U.S.A.   40
First Scholastic printing, July 1998

LOCATION: FIRST OFFICER'S QUARTERS/ CONSULAR SHIP TANTIVE IV

I'd like to be able to start at the beginning, but I don't have the luxury. We're about to exit from hyperspace at the planet Tatooine, and things are going to get busy.

So I have to start in the middle, and circle back to the beginning when I can. If you're reading the hard copy of this dictation, my advice is to get up to speed, fast. Look, I've never been a hand-holder type. My job is to get the facts down, and your job — whoever you are — is to get this account into the hands of the Rebellion. I promise a reward. Your help is vital to the Alliance.

Because if you're reading this, I'm most likely dead.

The facts: I boarded the Rebel ship *Tantive IV* in the Alderaan system. My mission had two objectives, both of them risky. First, the ship had to lurk in a restricted solar system, waiting for a crucial coded message.

Antilles, the commander of the *Tantive IV,* wasn't exactly thrilled to find himself hiding out in a system where he could get his ship overtaken by the Imperials. He didn't hesitate to say he thought this was a dangerous mission.

Captain Antilles has known me since I was a young girl on Alderaan, so he's not as respectful of my position as Senator and Princess as most people. He treats me as a comrade, and tells me exactly what he thinks. Usually, I appreciate his honesty. But that day, I could have done without it. I didn't need the distraction.

So I might have snapped when I told him bluntly that he didn't know what was at risk. Every nerve in my body was screaming, waiting for the coded communication to be transmitted. I had already sent the R2 unit to the navicomputer sensor suite. Under cover of doing repairs, the unit would receive the message.

Hundreds of Rebels had given their lives so this information could get through. I told Antilles as much as I strained toward the monitor.

Behind me, I could almost *hear* him fuming. His tone was frosty when he reminded me that he had the same security clearance as I did.

Of course he was right. And I trusted Antilles as much as my father, or myself. Sometimes, I have to admit, I don't like to share responsibility. It's easier to control outcomes when you're the only one accountable.

So I told him. This was the most important secret the Alliance had. On a recent mission, Antilles and I had heard a vague rumor about an Imperial strategic project called the Death Star. My father and I had discovered exactly what the project was — a massive space battle station as big as a moon. And it had the fire power to destroy whole *planets*.

When he heard that, Antilles's face went pale. He grasped right away what an awesome weapon that would be, and what it could do. He asked if it was online.

"Not yet," I told him.

But they were close. And the only chance the Alliance had was to get the technical readouts of the station. That was what I was waiting for. If Rebel strategists could find a flaw in the plans, we could find a way to destroy it.

Outside the spaceport, stars twinkled in galaxies light-years from us. Antilles and I gazed outside for a moment. Sometimes in space, you can feel like a tiny speck suspended in eternity.

"A space station the size of a moon," Antilles said softly.

He didn't have to tell me what he was thinking. I knew. Our small fleet was still in the process of getting organized. Our space pilots are all highly trained, but next to the size of the Imperial fleet, we were more of a nuisance than a threat.

But that's why the plans are so important! If a flaw is found, it might be all we need.

Besides, if there's one thing that boils my blood, it's someone throwing a doom-and-gloom scenario in my face. I'd heard them all before. *You can't fight the Imperials — they're too powerful. If you're a Senator, you can't run weapons behind the Emperor's back.*

It's too dangerous.

You'll get caught.

You'll lose.

I just can't listen to things like that. If I did, nothing would ever get done. The Rebellion doesn't have time to listen to odds.

Just then, the transmission static emitted a series of beeps. I leaned forward and punched the comlink. I told Artoo-Detoo to prepare to copy.

Antilles had chosen the R2 unit for me. The astromech droid was not only programmed for repairs and communication but could also re-sist interrogation probing. I could only hope the droid was up to the task ahead. I sent along his companion droid, See-Threepio, as an assis-tant. He would transmit Artoo's progress back to me through the comlink. He thought the R2 unit was doing normal duty repairs.

4

Now all I had to do was find the right frequency to decode the message. My fingers flew over the keys while Antilles suddenly strode to the navigation screen.

A starfleet cruiser was approaching. They'd found us! We had only minutes before they would demand we leave restricted space — or fire on us.

Antilles told me that we had to take evasive action. I refused. We had to delay!

The communications officer sounded nervous when he asked Antilles what to tell the Imperials. I had to sympathize. It had taken the Senate years of patient effort to draw up universal rules of engagement and communication in ship-to-ship encounters. The Imperials had destroyed them along with everything else that was decent and fair. They'd blast you just for not answering them quickly enough.

Antilles told the officer to tell the Imperials that he couldn't be located. He was seeing to repairs to the reactor. It was a smart move. It would give me a few minutes — if I was lucky — before they asked again. And it would keep them out of range, in case the reactor blew.

When I finally located the correct transmission code, I quickly punched the comlink and told Threepio to alert Artoo. About ninety seconds should do it.

But I guess I wasn't so lucky. The Imperials knew we were receiving a forbidden transmission. They demanded that Antilles release the boarding lock. Their laser guns were now aiming at us.

Antilles looked at me. We both knew the risk we were about to put the crew in. But we both knew the stakes. We had to continue.

Antilles's orders were crisp. "Repeat that we're a consular ship on a diplomatic mission. As soon as repairs are finished we'll be gone."

The communications officer was sweating now. The bridge was deadly quiet. None of the crew understood why we were putting the ship in such peril. We all knew the dangers of angering an Imperial warship ten times our size and firepower.

The Imperials sent a shuttle to the ship. I stared at the transmission record, my eyes burning. Hidden by the folds of my gown, my fingers were knotted in my lap. I didn't want the crew to see how nervous I was.

"They're ordering that I engage the boarding lock! Right *now*, sir!" The communications officer sounded frantic.

We were almost there. Only a few seconds remained. I gripped my hands together so hard I felt pain shoot up to my shoulder. The Imperials approached the docking bay.

Antilles came to stand behind my chair. He didn't say a word, or even look at me. We both watched the red indicator light of the transmission record.

It beeped, signaling the end of the transmission. Immediately, I barked an order into the comlink to Threepio. Get Artoo-Detoo out of the sensor suite and back aboard the ship! If we took off into hyperspace, he could be blown off the hull.

The infuriating protocol droid dithered on and on. I shouted at him to get moving.

Antilles anxiously gave the order to prepare to enter hyperspace. Meanwhile, the ship shuddered as the Imperials blasted our boarding lock.

Threepio's excited voice came over the comlink. Artoo was inside!

Okay, I admit it — we *did* cut it too close.

Antilles wheeled and gave the order to transmit to the Imperials that we had received an emergency transmission requiring our aid. "Hyperspeed," he told the navigator.

Stars rushed at us, and the galaxy became a memory in seconds. We had escaped them — barely. And no doubt our disobedience would be broadcast to other Imperial destroyers, who would be on the watch.

But we had the plans!

Antilles lowered himself into the chair next to me as though his bones hurt. He informed me that I'd just added ten years to his life.

That was Antilles — I had placed him in a tight spot, without any warning at all. And now, the information aboard his ship was putting every crew member in danger. But he could still take a moment to tease me.

He asked me what equally dangerous restricted area I wanted him to invade next.

"Tatooine," I told him.

I knew he'd be surprised. Why would we head to a remote planet in a far-off system?

He groaned and stood up. "Brief me later," he said. He'd had enough for one day. He headed off to examine his damaged boarding lock.

Well, it's better for only one of us to worry. Because once we get to Tatooine, my mission is to locate General Obi-Wan Kenobi. It won't be easy. Word is that after the Clone Wars, the Jedi Knight became a hermit.

And Tatooine is full of dangers. It's sparsely populated, mostly by moisture farmers and roving Jawa traders. The Sand People are ferocious scavengers, roaming the Jundland Wastes, where Obi-Wan was last seen living.

But finding General Kenobi isn't my biggest problem. Convincing him to join the Rebellion is. He gave everything of himself in the great battles of the Clone Wars. He's an old man now, and if anyone deserves peace, it is Obi-Wan. I will have to ask of him something I have no right to ask. But I will do it.

I can hear the engines reversing. We're coming out of hyperspace. I should get to the bridge. And then to Tatooine.

Wait — a battle station alert has just been announced over the speaker! What's going on?

Captain Antilles just told me the bad news over the comlink. We'll never make Tatooine now. The Imperials followed us through hyperspace. Even now, we're being pulled into the tractor beam of the *Devastator*. We're only minutes away from being boarded by Imperial troops. There must be a traitor on board who installed a tracking device, or broadcast our coordinates.

I'd like to catch the rat! But there's no time. We're being fired upon now. Antilles tried to outrun them, but the *Tantive IV* just doesn't have the power of a destroyer.

My mission is clear. I have to get the Death Star plans off this ship!

LOCATION: FIRST OFFICER'S QUARTERS/ CONSULAR SHIP TANTIVE IV

Okay, Leia, think. One thing I have a healthy respect for is Imperial thoroughness. If they search the ship, they'll not only find me — they'll find the R2 unit. Once they discover the plans are not in the ship's computer, they'll scan the memory banks of all the droids.

There has to be another way . . . .

The Imperials have jammed our communications. They'll also be watching for the launch of any escape pods. If life-forms are aboard, they'll blast them into nanospecs.

Life-forms . . .

But what about *droids*?

LOCATION: PORTSIDE
COMPANIONWAY

Captain Antilles accepted my plan. Trusting a droid might be risky — even reckless — but we have no choice. He ordered a full-scale resistance of the Imperial stormtroopers. They have already blasted their way through the boarding lock. They're aboard the ship.

I made my way to the labor pool in the tail of the ship. There, I located the R2 unit. I programmed the coordinates where we were likely to find General Kenobi on Tatooine. Then I recorded my holographic message. I asked for General Kenobi's help and explained that he must bring the R2 unit to Alderaan to be deprogrammed. *This is our most desperate hour,* I told him. *You're my only hope.*

I sent Artoo to the escape pods. Antilles will hold the bridge so that he can jettison the rest of the pods as soon as Artoo is off. It just might confuse the Imperials — they'll scan for life-forms. If none are aboard, they might assume it was a malfunction.

I know that the chances for success are slim. Not only will the droid have to escape the Imperial ships encircling the *Devastator*, it will have to locate Obi-Wan without being stolen or reprogrammed by farmers or Jawas on Tatooine.

But odds are mathematical formulas calculated to give people a reason not to try.

Smoke is beginning to fill the subhallways. The ship staggers with every blast. I can hear the sound of hand-to-hand fighting. The Imperials must be close.

I've kept my comlink open. Just now I heard a familiar voice ordering the stormtroopers to search the ship to locate me.

Darth Vader is aboard. This is not good news.

The Imperials must know something. Why else would the Dark Lord of the Sith chase a common transport ship? Could he know that I've obtained the Death Star plans?

So far, I've escaped Imperial imprisonment and interrogation. My position as a Senator gives me diplomatic immunity, and it's gotten me out of some tight spots in the past. I've been able to travel through the galaxy recruiting new members for the Rebellion, carrying supplies and weapons, and spoiling Imperial plans — all without getting caught.

But if Darth Vader finds me, I doubt I'll get away with diplomatic immunity this time. The Imperial warship wouldn't have acted this aggressively if they weren't convinced that the *Tantive IV* was a Rebel ship.

They're coming for me. I can only hide for so long.

Enough diplomacy. This time I'll meet Darth Vader with a blaster in my hand.

LOCATION: CREW QUARTERS/ IMPERIAL STAR DESTROYER DEVASTATOR

Captain Raymus Antilles is dead. He died bravely. Antilles refused to reveal any information about me or the Rebel Alliance. He insisted until his last breath that the *Tantive IV* was a consular ship on a diplomatic mission.

I couldn't hide from the stormtroopers for long. A squad found me and blasted me in stun mode. At least I managed to score a direct hit on one of them before they got me. If I have to take the Imperials down one at a time, I'll gladly do it.

They bound my hands and took me immediately to Darth Vader. I was still a little groggy from the blaster blow, but the sight of the Dark Lord of the Sith was enough to clear my head at once.

I've met him before. He's the one Imperial who can unnerve me. There is something disturbing about him, a dark energy like a chill wind that brings evil. It slapped me on both cheeks.

I won't let him intimidate me. I won't let him see my fear, or sense it. That's what he counts on. Fear. He's not going to get one ounce of it from me.

I didn't give him a chance to speak first. He doesn't deserve any diplomatic courtesy. I called him the Emperor's errand boy. I flung the words in his face like a taunt.

My aunts have always drilled into me the importance of making a good first impression.

He didn't react. He never does. Are there so many artificial parts holding him together that there's no man left in there?

He sounds more like a droid than a human, thanks to the mechanism in his breath-mask. In a toneless voice, he told me that I was a traitor and a Rebel spy. He had the stormtroopers take me away.

Now I'm being held in a crew cubicle aboard the *Devastator*. I have an uneasy feeling that Vader has special plans for me.

So you might say the situation is serious.

But all I can think about is Artoo-Deetoo. Our future is locked in his memory banks. And now that Antilles is dead, I'm the only one who knows that Artoo is on Tatooine.

My backup is this data recorder. My father, Viceroy Bail Organa, gave it to me back on

Alderaan. He wanted me to record my activities as a Senator for the Alderaan historical record. And he also told me that the act of recording my days would help me organize my thoughts and reflect on events.

Father is big on history and reflection.

But there will *be* no history to recount if the Imperials win! And reflection is a luxury I don't have time for. So I decided to use the diary to keep track of strategies and plans. It's a risk. If the Imperials find it, you can bet their codebreakers will be all over it like a flock of mynocks.

The design of the datapad is clever. It was fashioned on my home planet — Alderaan is well known for its innovative designers. It was originally designed for naturalists to carry on long journeys so that they could record their observations. It is capable of carrying billions of bits of voice data, can go for months without recharging, and is palm-sized and lighter than a hollow reed. It fits inside the buckle of my belt, and is undetectable by weapons or scanners.

In other words, it is perfect for my needs. I can keep a running record of Rebellion strategy.

So if the R2 unit doesn't reach General Kenobi, then this record will show that the technical readouts for the Death Star exist. Even if I'm captured, I can find a way to send it on its way. I've gone through too much; too many lives have been lost. The information must get through! For the sake of the Rebellion, and for the sake of Raymus Antilles.

Which reminds me. I had promised to circle back to the beginning. Now might be the best time.

I don't know what's ahead. But at least I can relate how I got here.

Antilles and I were on a mission to Ralltir when we first heard the words "Death Star." We were in a tight spot at the time.

We claimed to be on a mercy mission, carrying medical supplies. But actually, we were there to strengthen the Rebellion. We'd heard that many people on Ralltir were against the Empire, and their High Council was secretly sympathetic to the Alliance.

This was good news for us. Ralltir could become a powerful Rebel stronghold, but they needed our help. If we could bring field medical supplies and military hardware, they could hold out against the Imperial forces. The Ralltireans are known for their fierceness and integrity. Just what the Rebel Alliance needed.

So we landed on the planet, our hold full of turbo laser processors and field operations equipment. Unfortunately, the Imperial starfleet had reached the planet ahead of us. They declared a state of emergency, which meant we had to leave immediately. But first, Lord Tion, the Imperial task force commander, threatened to search our ship.

It was time to bluff, I told Antilles. I'd pull out my Princess bag of tricks and throw around words like "diplomatic mission" and "senatorial privilege." We'd be on our way in no time.

Antilles wasn't so sure. Tion wasn't the most clever official, but we shouldn't make the mistake of underestimating him. And Antilles had heard that Darth Vader was arriving to smash any resistance on Ralltir.

All the more reason to hurry, I argued. I could handle Lord Tion. At least I'd had dealings with him before. He'd briefly served on a committee in the Imperial Senate before he'd been given a position by the Emperor himself. Now he was one of the Imperial's rising young commanders — or should I say reptiles?

In the Empire, the scum always floats to the top. Just like in a toxic pond.

Antilles finally agreed to my plan. But he insisted on going with me to meet Lord Tion. Talk about a flesh-crawler. Tion oozed with politeness while he threatened us with search and seizure. I wished I could seize *him* — right around his scrawny neck!

But it became clear that Tion had an ulterior motive for his threats. In his warped mind, he thought that marrying a princess could help him gain power in the Imperial government.

Unfortunately, the princess he had in mind was me. If I agreed to meet him alone for dinner, he wouldn't search the ship.

Luckily, I didn't have to face such a sacrifice for the cause. A firefight broke out nearby, and we were ordered to leave the administration center. We were on our way to our landspeeder when we came across a wounded Rebel. He told us that the firefight was a diversion so that he could get to me. Hypnotically imprinted on his brain was information vital to the Alliance.

I didn't know it then, but that vital information was the existence of the Death Star battle station. All I knew at the time was that we had to get him away from Ralltir.

It wasn't easy. Especially when Darth Vader appeared. He suspected the firefight was a diversion, and was prepared to search not only the *Tantive IV*, but my landspeeder, which was where the wounded Rebel was hiding.

The Imperials were more concerned with the law then. Or should I say, concerned with the *appearance* of following the law. They were still trying to conquer parts of the universe with bribes and false promises. So they had to keep up their image.

I reminded Vader that Tion was in charge on

Ralltir, knowing that Vader would have to get Tion's permission to search. Everything must be done legally, so that there would be no questions in the Senate. He ordered us to wait.

Even I couldn't risk defying Darth Vader. Antilles and I were trapped.

It was the wounded Rebel who gave us the way out. He told us that the Imperials were about to enforce a full-scale surveillance of all communication in the administration center. Which meant that every word we spoke would be monitored and recorded.

You might say that was bad news. But I knew we could turn it to our advantage. If the Imperials wanted to snoop on our conversation, why not tell them what they wanted to hear?

I figured I couldn't go wrong counting on Tion's vanity. As soon as we knew we would be overheard, I told Antilles that if Tion searched my ship, my father would be furious, and forbid Tion to visit Alderaan.

Then again, if he *didn't* search the ship, I would know he was a true gentleman. I made sure to say this in a soft, gentle voice. Yes, I can manufacture a ladylike tone, if I have to. Even for an Imperial worm.

Antilles and I exchanged a wordless glance. Would Tion fall for the ruse? Would he be stupid enough to let us go?

We were on our way in minutes.

Later, back on Alderaan, Father and I discussed what to do next. Thanks to the Rebel, who recovered from his wounds, we now knew about the Death Star. What we needed was more information.

And someone stupid enough to give it to us. Someone who would be puffed up by flattery. Someone who would want to impress us.

Lord Tion reappeared just in time.

At first, I was irritated that I was forced to entertain him. But perhaps an intimate family dinner was just the thing. We served all of Alderaan's delicacies. And I promised my father I would be polite. That was the way to get information out of the womp rat.

A little flattery did the trick. Right after he proposed marriage to me — and my food made a somersault in my stomach — Tion began to boast about a secret ultimate weapon.

Foolishly, he let a crucial piece of information slip. The detailed plans of the Death Star would be on the next transport, heading for the Imperial vaults.

Okay, I admit it — right here, I made a stupid mistake. My excuse is that Tion drove me over the edge. He was so arrogant! So sure of the Empire's power. It made me furious.

I slipped and called the project the "Death Star." Tion knew I had to be a Rebel, that there was no other way for me to know the code name. He drew his blaster. But he didn't expect resistance from a princess.

Sometimes, it's helpful to be underestimated.

I threw myself at Tion. We struggled for his blaster. It went off, and he died.

I have no remorse. In his role as task force commander, Tion had been responsible for the death and suffering of whole populations. He would have gone on to inflict more misery on the innocent. I think of those people when I remember that moment.

Father and I got word to the Rebel base, and a great battle was launched. Many of our men died. But the plans were captured. They were broadcast to me on the *Tantive IV*.

The rest you know.

Now, I wait for Vader to send for me. This is the first time he's called me an out-and-out traitor. And my killing a stormtrooper hasn't exactly helped my claim that I'm only a Senator.

But I think my best bet is to bluff my way out. No matter how hard Vader will try to intimidate me. I'll continue to act as though the authority of the Senate is behind me. Vader has no real proof. And there's a big difference between having Rebel sympathies and being an active Rebel agent. If he can prove that I'm an agent, he'll claim that he has the right to imprison me.

Besides, if I keep insisting that I'm merely a Senator despite all the evidence to the contrary, it just might infuriate Vader. Now *that's* a pleasant thought.

I've coiled my hair into the style of the royal house of Alderaan. I've arranged my garments and tried to clean up as much as possible. Now I sit in my most chillingly regal of poses.
I'm ready to face the Dark Lord.

LOCATION: CREW QUARTERS/ DEVASTATOR/ORBITING THE DEATH STAR STATION

I've seen it. I've seen the Death Star. Tion, for once, did not exaggerate. It is huge, as big as a class-four moon. Evil emanates from it like an icy wave.

Darth Vader brought me to the viewport. He stood close by, watching my face as I caught my first glimpse. I could tell that he wanted me to be frightened by the sight of it.

So I told him that I was sorry to disappoint him. If he wanted me to faint at the sight of Imperial magnificence, I just wasn't the type.

Besides, the bigger the Imperial weapons grow, the more pathetic they seem.

His breathing wheezed behind me. The sound froze my blood. I'd heard that when they hear it, even the cruelest Imperial warriors scurry for cover.

"Brave words for a princess without a throne to hide behind," Vader told me. He added that my days of protection were over. I was a traitor and a spy, and that's how I'd be treated.

I suggested that he check with the Emperor before he made any more decisions. After all, rumor had it that he was incapable of making a move without his boss's approval.

He didn't answer. His breath was audible behind the mask. I stared back into the eyes of the helmet, eyes like a giant insect. Blank. Black. Emotionless.

My battle of wills with Vader is also a battle of nerves. He is more powerful than I am — for now. But I'll never let him know that I know it. Bravado can substitute for bravery at times.

He has me at a disadvantage. I am his prisoner. I think my best tactic will be to show contempt for his authority with every word, every breath. I'll match him, taunt for taunt. I consider keeping Darth Vader off balance a personal challenge!

He told me that the Death Star was our destination. But I'd already guessed as much.

"And if you don't cooperate, it could be your last resting place," he said.

I told myself to keep cool. Losing my temper or shouting would please him too much. So I turned my back on him. I told him that he had just threatened a member of the Imperial Senate. It was a punishable offense.

Of course, I was bluffing. The Emperor would never punish Darth Vader, and we both knew it.

He sighed, as if I bored him. He told me I was wasting my breath, and his time. He signaled to his men, and they took me below.

So I'm back in a crew cubicle, waiting. Vader thinks that a prison term on the Death Star is a frightening punishment. But he's wrong.

Bringing me to the Imperial's best-kept secret could turn out to be a fatal mistake. I'm about to get a closeup view of their most formidable weapon. I just might be able to help the Rebellion more on the Death Star than anywhere else.

And now my diary will become even more important. My eyes and ears will be open. I'll record every observation. I'll count troops and transports and weapons. And if I can't leave the station, I'll make sure the diary survives and finds a way into the hands of the Rebellion.

There are no spaceports in this cube, but I can hear the noise of docking activity.

We have landed on the Death Star.

LOCATION: DETENTION BLOCK AA 23/ DEATH STAR

I'm now being held in a detention block, in a locked cell. I wasn't given a chance to protest. I was shoved inside, and the door hissed behind me.

We landed in a huge docking bay, the biggest I've ever seen on a space station. I counted at least fifty TIE fighters lined in take-off formation. There must be more. I think there are additional hangars all around the docking bay. Guards hurried me past three large transport ships being unloaded.

We traveled down a long corridor that snaked off the docking bay at a right angle. After approximately a hundred yards, we took a right turn. The airlift was another hundred yards or so down a well-used corridor.

The space station may not be fully operational yet, but it's loaded with staff. I saw squads of Imperial stormtroopers as well as ranking officers. There were also technicians and other personnel. Everyone seemed very busy.

My impression is that the Death Star is a multileveled station that's built around a central core. There could even be air passages in that core, so that ships can move from one quad to another.

The airlift opened directly into the prisoners' dock. A command center sat immediately in front of the doors. I believe it's the only exit from the dock, so escape would have to take that into account. The center was manned by four stormtroopers and one main guard at the central post. The locking devices are located there. Next time I'm led out from the cell, I'll count again, to see if the number of guards is standard or unusual.

Now I have to wait and watch for my chance to escape. Already I've discovered that it's exactly five paces from one end of my cell to another. My bunk is adequate, but I can get no rest. Inactivity has always been difficult for me, despite my aunts' attempt to drill patience into my nature. Back on Alderaan, Tia, Rouge, and Celly would say, "All action is foolish without reflection. Wait and learn, Leia — and learn how to wait."

"I don't have time to wait!" I would cry. "I can learn while I go."

But now here I am, waiting. All I can think about is the success of that little droid. How can he find his way to General Kenobi in the vast Jundland Wastes?

I had to pause. My breath just left me. My heart suddenly seemed to expand, and a powerful feeling came over me. It came from deep within me. It spoke, but it had no voice.

It told me that Artoo will succeed. That Obi-Wan Kenobi will be reached.

I don't know where the feeling came from. I've never felt anything like it. It reminds me of tales my father told me of the Jedi Knights, of the element they call the Force. Something that surrounds us and binds us to everything in the universe.

I feel a new strength in my body, a new defiance in my mind. It is almost as though Obi-Wan himself has told me to hang on.

It doesn't matter if it came from Obi-Wan, or from something in me. I can use it. I can—

LOCATION: PRISONER'S DOCK/DEATH STAR

I've rewound the data tape here so I can in-dicate that as Darth Vader entered my cell, I hid my recorder and kept it running:

Vader: Ah, Princess Leia. Sorry to disturb your rest. You'll need it here. Your interroga-tion sessions won't be pleasant, I'm afraid.

Leia: Vader, I demand to know on what au-thority I am being held in a prison cell. What crime have I committed? Or rather, what charge have you *manufactured* to keep me here? Once the Imperial Senate hears of this —

Vader: There is no one to protest, Princess Leia. The Emperor has abolished the Imperial Senate.

Leia: This is outrageous! Not to mention against the Council Rules of Order. The Em-peror has shown contempt for our laws, it's true, but this is going too far, even for him.

Vader: I am not interested in your opinions, Princess Leia. I'm interested in the Death Star plans. What have you done with them?

Leia: I don't know what you mean. And I'm tired of being asked the same question repeatedly. Now, if you don't mind —

Vader: We're tracking those droids on Tatooine. It's only a matter of time before we find them. You look dismayed, Princess Leia.

Leia: Hardly. If you want to chase a couple of droids across the galaxy, be my guest. But I have to say, I'm confused. I find it puzzling that you're so intent on finding these plans. You yourself told me that the Death Star station is invincible. So why should you care about the plans?

Vader: Don't trifle with me, Princess —

Leia: Wait, I'm really trying to understand this. It's such a lapse in logic. And don't you pride yourself on your logic, Vader? Could Darth Vader be growing irrational? You *are* under pressure . . . . Licking the Emperor's boots can be so tiring.

Vader: It is you who are irrational if you expect to continue to bluff. Talk all you wish, if it amuses you. We will find out everything you know in time. Including the location of the hidden Rebel base.

Leia: Do you need a new hearing device in that helmet, Vader? I've already told you — I was engaged on a mission of diplomacy. Perhaps you've heard the term?

I can see that I need to explain the concept. It's when life-forms use *intelligence* and *reason* to solve their differences. Unfamiliar concepts for the Imperials, I admit — but the rest of the universe depends on them. Which is why the Empire will fall, in the end.

Vader: You disappoint me, Princess Leia. Taunts and threats are the weapons of a child.

Leia: I am a Senator of the Imperial Court! I *demand* my freedom. When my father, Viceroy Bail Organa of Alderaan, hears of this —

Vader: I'm afraid your father cannot help you, Princess. The *Tantive IV* has been blown to space dust. I have made sure that word has gone out that none aboard survived. Your father thinks you are dead.

That scream and the scuffling noise you just heard? That was when I lost my temper.

I couldn't help myself. The thought of my father's grief sent me over the edge. Hot rage pumped through my body, and I threw myself at Vader.

I wanted to rip that breath-mask from his head. I wanted to see his eyes, see the real man — the animal — underneath the helmet. I wanted to expose him. I wanted to kill him.

I caught him by surprise, and my fingers found the ridge under the collar of his helmet. I almost succeeded in yanking it off. But he pushed me away. His strength is extraordinary. Some extra force seemed to propel me, and I flew backward across the cell and slammed into the wall.

That loud noise at the end of the scuffling was the sound of me hitting the wall. My recorder shut off with the impact. I'm lucky it didn't break.

What am I saying? I'm lucky my *head* didn't break.

My ears rang as I watched Vader raise a gloved fist. I stared at him, daring him to strike me.

But his fist fell to his side. Vader stood over me, just breathing for a moment. Usually, it's hard to tell when someone wearing a helmet is angry at you. But I got the distinct feeling that the Dark Lord was fuming.

Good. Let him be mad.

He sounded completely calm when he told me that I would regret what I'd done. Perhaps a session with an Imperial interrogator droid would teach me the importance of respect.

Then he left, the door hissing closed behind him.

I've heard whispers about these droids —

torture devices invented by twisted Imperial minds. It is said that they can deliver unimaginable pain. Pain so intense that it has never been experienced before — worse than pain from any disease or wound known in the universe. That is why the Imperials use droids — there's no danger of human mercy entering the picture.

But I can stand it, if it comes. I've seen the Imperials inflict horrible pain on civilizations across the galaxy. I've seen their "purification" methods. If others can bear it, so can I.

But why wait for it? Escape always *seems* impossible — until it works. Is this Death Star as security-tight as it appears?

I've decided to test it. If I can manage to get out of the dock, I can hide in the main hangar. Those transports I saw must come and go frequently in a station this big. There might be a chance to slip aboard with cargo.

It won't be easy. The prisoners' dock is manned by a combination of stormtroopers and regular security troops. They are a follow-orders kind of bunch, who don't think for themselves, so I might be able to trick them.

My great advantage is surprise. They would not expect someone like me to try to escape. I've thought of several ideas, gone over them in my head. But I've decided the simplest plan is the best.

LOCATION: PRISONERS' DOCK/DEATH STAR

I waited until the guard arrived with food. I stood in the middle of the cell, waiting for him. He was surprised, I could tell, to find me in his face as soon as the door hissed open.

I had hoped that the food handler wouldn't be a stormtrooper from the elite guard, but a rank and file trooper. Someone used to following orders. I was lucky.

"I demand to see Darth Vader," I said. "I am Princess Leia of Alderaan. I know the Emperor personally, and I must see Vader. *Now.*"

He placed the food tray down in the slot by the bunk. I could almost see his small brain ticking. What should he do? Ignore me, and suffer the consequences? Or obey me, and possibly have the wrath of Darth Vader on his head? Should he call a superior? Yes, that was it.

It wasn't hard to read him. Imperial soldiers always want to pass the buck.

"I demand . . . to see Darth Vader," I said, weakening my voice and making it falter. "I —"

And then I fell to the ground.

That was the hard part — to relax my muscles, force my body to topple without breaking my fall. I've never been good at giving up control. My head hit the floor with a crack, bringing tears to my eyes. But I stayed still as death while the guard shouted at me to rise. I didn't flinch when he kicked me — I have a purple bruise to show for it.

But the next time his boot came down, I grabbed it. I yanked it hard, and he fell. I didn't expect a guard to be quite so foolish, but you can never underestimate the basic stupidity of one of the Emperor's mind-followers.

I knew from my encounter with Vader that I should hook my fingers under the lip of the guard's helmet. I wrenched it off and then used it like a club to smash him on the head.

That allowed me the one second I needed to grab his blaster. It was on stun. I blasted him, then deactivated the door with his device. I slipped out, leaving the guard inside.

The hallway was empty. It was narrow, and the walls curved above my head. I studied it for a moment. There didn't appear to be tracking devices in the ceiling. Good.

Gripping the blaster, I moved cautiously toward the control center. As I moved, I followed through on the plan I'd formulated in my cell. As I passed each cell, I activated the release lock. If I released all the prisoners, the guards at the command center would have their hands full. In the confusion, I might be able to slip away and get to the docking bay.

But I hadn't expected all the cells to be empty.

I almost groaned aloud. How could it be? If there was one thing the Imperials were good at, it was arresting innocent people. I realized that the Death Star was too new yet to have prisoners. So I was their first. What a treat.

I moved faster now. It wouldn't take the guard at the center long to wonder why the cell doors were opening. Cell checks or cleaning were probably scheduled. And someone would be starting to worry about the food handler by now.

By the time I reached the end of the corridor, I was running. Unfortunately, I almost ran into a squad of stormtroopers, who suddenly appeared in front of me.

My blaster was at the ready, and I got off two good shots. I took down two stormtroopers before they got me. I think I must have been hit three times.

At least their blasters were on stun. I guess Vader wants to keep me alive — for now. When I came to, I was back in my cell. My food had been removed, I guess as punishment. I was bruised, and I had a headache the size of a Yavin moon.

At least I learned something — my cell number. I heard a guard call it out when they were still trying to figure out what was going on. It's not much, and probably won't help me at all, but I record it here: 2187.

It didn't take long for Darth Vader to appear in my doorway. I must be a nice sharp thorn in his side. A cheerful thought.

"Your pathetic attempts at resistance grow tiresome," Vader told me. "But you will bore me no further."

He announced that interrogation would no longer be delayed. It would begin today. He retreated, his cape flicking like the wings of a rabid swamp bat. The door hissed closed.

So I'm scheduled for a torture session with the Imperial interrogator droid! But Vader made the mistake of telling me. He will have no element of surprise. And I have time to prepare.

I've had training on Alderaan. There are mind methods to help one withstand torture. The technique involves what the masters call a "drawing inward," using breathing and visualization techniques. I must think of brain-images that will keep my mind aloof from the pain. I must separate mind and body so that I will not reveal a single secret. I must stay in each moment, not anticipating the pain to come or reliving the pain from the moment before.

The one drawback to the technique is that, on peaceful Alderaan, no one could bear to actually cause pain. So I practiced techniques while holding ice in both my hands, or being subjected to extreme cold or loud noises for short periods of time. I was able to free my mind from feeling anything under these conditions.

But I have a feeling the interrogator droid won't hand me two ice cubes to hold. Vader will have something a little more extreme in mind.

Okay, I'll be honest. With the thought of torture facing me, I'd rather be anywhere but here. But if I can manage to stay focused and not reveal even the most trivial secret, Darth Vader will lose face with the Imperial high command. I'll be able to have that one small pleasure. With that, and the thought of the great Rebellion, I'll bear anything they throw at me.

EIGHTH ENTRY

LOCATION: PRISONERS' DOCK/CELL 2187/ DEATH STAR

I'm weak. And dizzy. It's hard to speak or even to lift my head. I can't make it to my cot. I'm lying on the floor.

Like an animal. This is what they did to me.

I try not to feel hatred. Because that's what they want. Hatred weakens the spirit as pain weakens the body.

I didn't think such pain existed. In *any* universe.

I have to rest now. To prepare for next time. But I record this fact:

He . . . did not . . . break me.

LOCATION: PRISONERS' DOCK/CELL 2187/ DEATH STAR

The torture began with one needle. It probed my most sensitive nerves. Darth Vader stood by. The pain grew until I broke my promise not to scream and let out a cry that came from the deepest part of myself.

I practiced my mind techniques in the beginning. But as the pain began to take over, I could no longer reason properly. And then, as my sanity was slipping away, Vader spoke to me. He spoke in the voice of a friend. He wanted to end my pain — didn't I want it to end, too? It would be so easy. It would happen immediately. He was my friend. All he had to do was raise his hand. And all I had to do was reveal where the Death Star plans were, or the location of the hidden Rebel base. Either piece of information would bring me sweet relief.

I held on.

"Never," I gritted out. Just that one word cost me a great effort.

The needle probed deeper. The pain grew and grew until I lost consciousness. They revived me.

And then they started all over again.

More pain. More terror.

I would have broken if I hadn't been trained so well. I clung to the pieces of my training that had been shattered by the pain. Vader used the Force, trying to convince me that he was working for the Rebellion. That my father wanted me to reveal the location of the hidden base. Didn't I want to please my father?

Confused and in raging pain, I held out against that voice. In the end, my resistance became nothing more than a single point of consciousness. A pinprick of light illuminating the darkness around me. I had to hold on to that pinprick. I concentrated and concentrated on that tiny particle of light, knowing that if I let it go—all was lost.

Then from somewhere far away, I heard Vader's voice. I heard him say, "Enough."

He wanted me alive. They would try again later.

My eyes were closed, and my grip on consciousness was weak. But I heard the hiss of the door with relief.

I'd made it through.

They've let me rest, at least. I can stretch out on my bunk, my head propped against the wall. It helps with the dizziness. Every so often over the past twenty-four hours or so, I've felt a shudder against my skull. At first, I thought it was the aftereffect of the torture. But I realize now it's some function of the Death Star.

What could it be? Now that I think about it, I've heard thumps, too, over the course of my time here. And at times, my cell doesn't smell very pleasant. There's a faint odor to the air, of something rotten, something foul. An occasional stench that manages to invade the antiseptic walls.

The garbage chute! I'm next to the garbage chute. The Imperials must process their waste right next to the prisoner's dock. It makes sense — they wouldn't put a smelly refuse processor next to the commanders' quarters.

They've created a mighty killing station, but they can't disguise their own stench!

I think it's night. But I can't sleep, knowing that I may have to face the torture again. I must prepare myself. I must push away the fear that makes my body feel liquid. I truly don't know if I can withstand a second session so soon.

It's time to face the possibility of my death. If they come for me tomorrow, I could break. I was taught on Alderaan that it is my duty to assess my strength honestly, and not overestimate what I'm capable of.

If my mind is broken by Vader, I would endanger the entire Rebellion. Which means there is only one option — to die before they learn anything.

So first, I'll try to fight. That might force them to kill me. And I'll try to take as many stormtroopers down with me as I can. Better yet, an officer. Or Vader himself!

But if fighting is impossible, I'll have to will myself to die. I know how to do this. I've been taught this, too. It's said to be the most difficult mind-act there is, especially if you are young and healthy. But I know above all else that the Rebellion is worth dying for. That should help me.

I don't know for sure if I can succeed. But I'll do everything humanly possible. I can't let the Rebellion down.

I've found a small crack between my bunk and the wall. I'm going to leave the data pad there, in hopes that some future prisoner will find it. Maybe he or she will have better luck, and will escape.

If you find this, bring it to Alderaan, to my father, Viceroy Bail Organa. He will reward you.

Father, the R2 unit must be protected. The information must be passed along.

I know that you will grieve for me. But we both believe in things greater than ourselves. What is one life compared to the great struggle?

Father, know that I died thinking of you, and of freedom.

Princess Leia of Alderaan

LOCATION: PRISONERS'
DOCK/CELL 2187/
DEATH STAR

I mark this day. It will live in my mind forever. My home planet Alderaan is gone.

Millions of lives vaporized. My father, my best friend Winter, my aunts, my teachers, my friends. All gone. An entire civilization vanished from the galaxy in an instant of heat, of light.

When they came for me, I had expected further torture. I would have borne it gladly. But not this.

Anything but this.

Darth Vader came for me with a squad of troopers. They bound my hands and kept their blasters at the ready. I didn't ask any questions. I was gathering myself for the next torture session. I guessed that they were bringing me to one of their infamous "interrogation rooms."

But instead, I was brought to the main observation deck. I was ushered into the presence of Grand Moff Tarkin himself.

I had met him before. We'd had numerous clashes in the Senate, before the Emperor rewarded him with a military command. Governor Tarkin is known for his cunning and his ruthlessness. His skin is gray, as though there isn't blood running through his veins, but a vile toxic fuel. He's more like a machine than a man — like Vader, but without the helmet and breath-mask.

Tarkin got things rolling by informing me that he'd signed my death order. If he thought this would frighten me, he was wrong. I had expected it. I was ready to meet death, if it came. More ready than they knew.

But then he surprised me. I expected him to question me about the hidden Rebel base. I was prepared to play the same cat-and-mouse game with him as I did with Vader. After a torture droid, Tarkin would be child's play, I figured.

But Tarkin turned out to be the cruelest of all my tormentors.

He directed my attention to the viewscreens. I recognized the blue world spinning in the middle of the most beautiful star constellation in a thousand galaxies. Alderaan.

Tarkin told me that if I didn't reveal the site of the Rebel base, he would test the Death Star's destructive power on my home planet. He would blow it up.

The look in his gray eyes chilled me to the bone. It wrenched a cry from my throat. I told him that Alderaan was a peaceful planet. We had even outlawed weapons.

Tarkin was unmoved. Would I prefer a military target? Then name it. Where was the Rebel base?

Who would I condemn to die? Innocent children, men and women who were leading their lives peacefully, securely, on my own home planet? Or soldiers?

I saw satisfaction in Tarkin's gaze. He had me, he knew it — and he triumphed in it.

I stared at the blue planet. I couldn't let it be destroyed! I couldn't just stand there and watch! If I had to see that, I'd die right there.

But I couldn't betray my comrades, either.

There was another option. Only one. I had to delay them. And in the meantime, I could escape, or be killed, or manage to outwit them somehow. Alderaan would be spared, because what would be the point of destroying it if they couldn't use it to gain information from me?

"Dantooine," I said. The planet was the location of an old base, in a remote outer system. It would take them time to discover that we had abandoned the base there some time ago. We never stayed in one place very long. "They're on Dantooine." My voice was a whisper, as if it had been wrenched out of me. I wasn't faking. I had been shaken by Tarkin's threat.

Then, in a voice that will live in my nightmares, I heard Tarkin give the order to fire.

He had double-crossed me! I watched helplessly as a laser shot out into space and connected with Alderaan. The planet exploded into space dust in a split second.

It was like a giant hand had squeezed my heart, compacting it into a solid ball of pain. I staggered. My ears were filled with a great cry, as if I could hear the screams . . . .

I closed my eyes and tried to control my emotions. *Not now, Leia,* I told myself. *Don't give them the satisfaction of seeing you break.*

We had been told that the Death Star had the capability to destroy whole planets. But in my heart, I hadn't totally believed it. Fear is a weapon used by the Imperials to keep subjects in line. They use lies to confuse and threaten. And even if they *had* the power, would they use it?

Now I knew that their evil knew no human bounds. It was that black.

I turned on Tarkin and Vader. "You have only shown me the seeds of your own destruction."

I said. "You have no souls. That's why your Empire is doomed. And that's why the Rebellion *will* succeed. Now I'm sure of it!"

Then, they dragged me away.

I am to be executed. But when I close my eyes, all I can see is the white light of Alderaan's destruction against my eyelids.

I never want that white light to fade. I never want to forget.

Last night, I decided to will myself to die. But after this, I refuse.

I don't know yet how I can escape this station of death, but I vow that I will. And then the real battle will begin. Not for vengeance — for justice.

I'll see Vader and his Emperor die before my very last breath. I will never give up!

LOCATION: CARGO COMPARTMENT B2 ON THE MILLENNIUM FALCON

Here is proof that when a just cause is involved, the impossible becomes possible. I have escaped. I am on a ship called the *Millennium Falcon*, just gone into hyperspace, speeding toward the Rebel base.

The R2 unit is aboard. Soon, the plans will be analyzed, and the attack will be launched.

I've found an empty cargo hold to be alone and record the details of my escape. It seems strange to be aboard this junk heap of a ship, pushed up against an old crate, sneezing from the dust. My cell on the Death Star is far away now.

I fought my way out of the Death Star side by side with two strangers. Their names are Luke Skywalker and Han Solo. We were helped by the two droids — Artoo-Detoo and that chattering See-Threepio. Artoo turned out to be resourceful and . . . well, *clever,* if I can give a human quality to a droid. Antilles chose well when he picked him.

Then there is the Wookiee named Chewbacca. He looks like a walking fur coat with mange. But believe me, I was so glad to hear that Artoo had been located that I would have kissed Chewbacca, if I could have found his lips.

The most insignificant of my rescuers is the Corellian smuggler, Han Solo. Okay, he's handy in a fight. I give him that. But he counts too much on his handsome looks and big talk. I've known him less than a day, and I've already figured out that nobody could be as big a fan of Han Solo as Han Solo himself.

He has no interest in a cause — his honor can be bought and sold. Money is his goal. His ship is as disreputable as he is. At least I've bought his cooperation for as long as I need it.

Luke Skywalker, the second stranger, is younger, about my age. When he burst into my cell back on the Death Star, I wasn't exactly impressed. And my doubt increased instantly — as stormtroopers began firing at us. He and Captain Solo hadn't bothered to formulate an escape plan. They had no clue about how to get off the prisoner's dock — much less the Death Star!

The last member of the party was Obi-Wan Kenobi. And now I must record the sad news.

My heart is heavy as I say this: Obi-Wan Kenobi is dead. He sacrificed himself to make sure the rest of us got away. Luke is especially saddened by the loss. I'm sorry, Luke.

I still can't quite believe it either . . . .

Let me go back to my last data entry. After I left Tarkin and Vader, all I wanted to do was *act*. I was ready to take on the whole Imperial army singlehandedly. I wanted to avenge my family and my world. But I knew I needed sleep. I was determined to escape, and rest might not come for a long time.

So I lay down in my bunk, and I thought about Alderaan. I couldn't think about Father or my aunts — that hurt too much. So I thought about the green fields and the blue flowers, and my favorite walk through the hills. Remembering was a way of avenging, I told myself. Someday, after the downfall of the Empire, I would set down a record of my world.

I fell asleep, thinking of how beautiful Alderaan was. I awoke at the sound of the door hissing open. A stormtrooper stood there, gaping at me.

I was instantly awake, and afraid. I assumed he was there to escort me to another torture session. But I pretended nonchalance. I pointed out that he seemed a little short, for a stormtrooper.

To my shock, the trooper lifted off his helmet. Electric blue eyes blazed at me across the room. The thought rushed through my brain that this was *definitely* not an Imperial.

It was Luke Skywalker. He confidently announced that he had come to rescue me. Sweet relief flooded through me — at last, action! I sprang up, ready for anything. Little did I know I was about to be trapped under blaster fire in a corridor.

Did I mention that Han and Luke were a little short on strategy? Well, it bears repeating.

Introductions to Captain Solo and Chewbacca were made under laser fire. Things didn't look good. We were trapped and outnumbered, and wouldn't be able to hold out for long. But just then I remembered the garbage chute I'd heard rumbling by my cell. I grabbed Luke's blaster and fired it at the wall so we could all drop through the opening into the chute.

You'd think Han Solo would thank me for saving his skin. Instead, he started grumbling about the smell of the place. As if a garbage chute would smell like t'iil blossoms!

But the smell was the least of our problems. It turned out that we weren't alone in that garbage soup. Something rippled under the water — something alive. And *big*.

Luke was suddenly sucked underneath the surface. He barely had time to let out a cry. A slimy creature had wrapped its tentacle around his throat, and Han and I couldn't loosen its grip.

Luke was sucked underwater, and I thought we'd lost him. In shock, I stared at the murky water. Was I about to see more death, so soon?

Suddenly, the walls of the chute shuddered with the same groaning noise I'd heard in my cell. Luke shot to the surface, gasping. The creature had simply let him go. But why?

We got our answer when, with a terrifying groan, the walls began to move. We were in the compactor!

I didn't have time to feel afraid. We grabbed beams, pieces of metal, any debris we could find. We tried to brace them against the walls. But nothing worked. The walls just snapped the metal beam in two like a twig. Soon, it would do the same to our bones.

Han and I shared a desperate glance. I saw no fear in his face — just exasperation. I felt the same. After all that struggle, would my life end in a pile of Imperial garbage? The sheer unfairness of it made me angry, and I pounded a fist against the groaning wall.

Then, just as we thought it was over, just as

we were about to be flattened so thin you could slip us under a door, Luke raised Artoo and Threepio on the comlink. Artoo shut down the compactor mechanism. The groaning walls stopped.

We cheered, laughed, stomped our feet in the garbage. Han and I hugged. I don't know why. Except that he was there. When I pulled away, I saw surprise on his face, as though he were surprised to find that I was a human, not a droid.

Artoo unlocked the hatch, and we scrambled out, dripping and smelling like womp rats.

While I shook out my gown, I asked Luke to fill me in. He told me that there was a ship waiting in the docking bay. They'd left the R2 unit waiting in a guard room.

I was furious. Artoo was more important than any of us! How could he have left him? Threepio was hardly adequate protection. The thought of crucial Death Star plans roaming around an Imperial ship made my blood run cold.

We had to get to the main docking bay as fast as possible. Luke told me that Obi-Wan was on a mission to dismantle the tractor beam for our getaway.

At least *someone* had a decent plan.

*　　　*　　　*

Dodging a space station full of stormtroopers isn't easy. The rush toward the docking bay couldn't be a straight line. We had to double back several times in order to avoid troops.

As we made our way through the corridors, I decided that if the Wookiee's bellowing and Captain Hotshot's blasting didn't give us away, it would be a miracle. What good is Solo's bravery if he takes risks without thinking? And most maddening of all, he didn't seem to realize that I was in charge. This was my mission — not his!

I had to inform him that, contrary to what he might think, he had to do what I said.

He didn't take it well. He practically snarled at me insisting he didn't take orders from anybody but himself. Obviously he needed some *more* talking to. But we had to keep moving. I didn't have time to put him in his place as firmly as I'd like.

We made it to an overlook on the main docking bay. That's when I got my first glimpse of Captain Solo's beloved ship. Heap of space junk is more like it. The poor *Falcon* looked thoroughly clumsy and rundown next to the gleaming Imperial transports.

Han was furious when I asked him if he'd really made it to the Death Star in that thing. *You're braver than I thought,* I told him.

Okay. Maybe it wasn't a great idea to insult my ride home. One of these days I'll figure out how to think before I speak.

We were close to the hangar when we had to split up. Luke and I headed off on our own. As we were trying to escape from a couple of stormtroopers, we stumbled into a very tight spot. We nearly fell into an abyss as we landed on a small platform over the central core shaft.

Luke blasted the control panel, closing the hatch door just in time. But he also blasted our only means of escape — controls to the retractable bridge. We were trapped, and exposed on the ledge. Troopers were seconds away from getting the hatch open. More troopers appeared across the shaft.

It was at that moment that I first felt something odd. Something that connected me to this stranger, Luke Skywalker. A feeling that's only grown stronger over the short time I've known him.

First of all, he reacted exactly as I would have. The thought of giving up never crossed his mind. I guess he doesn't believe in impossible odds, either.

Luke handed me his blaster. But I *knew* he was going to, before he did. My hands were ready to take it. He found a grappling hook on his belt, and threw it across the shaft. While I fired at the troopers, he made the rope fast.

Before he reached for me, I was ready. Our arms went around each other's waists. I kissed him on the cheek — for luck. It was an impulse I'd never felt before — to kiss a stranger. We flew across the shaft, our muscles perfectly in sync.

We made it to the docking bay. Han and Chewbacca were seconds behind us. But we had one last obstacle: Darth Vader. That's when Obi-Wan gave his life for us. In a lightsaber battle with Vader, he simply let his saber fall. In the confusion, we escaped aboard the ship.

Or did we escape?

I suspect that our escape was not so lucky. I'm convinced that the Imperials let us go. They just made it *look* hard. Once we made it aboard the ship, they sent their TIE fighters to shoot at us. Han and Luke fought bravely, but they could have shot like amateurs, and it wouldn't have mattered. Vader didn't want any direct hits.

He wanted to follow us. I know it. I feel it. There's a tracking beam aboard the *Millennium Falcon*.

So right now, I'm leading the Imperials to our base. To where our entire fleet, our most brilliant military minds, are quartered.

It's a risk. That's why I'm continuing with this journal. Until I've safely delivered the plans and the Death Star is a bad memory, I'll continue to record our progress. Nothing must be left to chance.

The next stop is the fourth moon of Yavin. I have no choice. If the Death Star follows us, it will just make destroying it that much easier. If it's allowed to be fully operational, we are all doomed.

The time for attack is now.

TWELFTH ENTRY

LOCATION: MILLENNIUM FALCON/NAVIGATION CENTER

I can't wait to get off this bucket of bolts! I've just been to the bridge to confer with the pilot and copilot. They should know that the Death Star is on our tail. When we come out of hyperspeed, we'll have to act fast.

I'm actually beginning to like that furball, Chewbacca. There's something brave and kind in his eyes.

But Captain Solo is another matter. When I told him that I thought the Imperials had let us go in order to track us, he just laughed at me. "Leave the strategy to me, sweetheart," he said.

Is the guy *asking* me to strangle him?

I don't know why I expected a different response. Like something close to intelligence. And I can't stand the way he twists my title. If I hear another "Your Highnessness" or "Your Worshipfulness," I'll scream.

Yes, I grew up in the royal house of Alder-aan. But I wasn't the least bit pampered. On Alderaan, royalty is a title of service, not privi-lege. My training stressed my service to my planet and to others, and involved an extensive learning period. I was taught the basics of preparing food, making garments, and tending gardens — as well as state diplomacy, ad-vanced communications, and weapons skills.

Not that I'll tell Captain High and Mighty Solo these things. Obviously, his major interest in life is himself. He —

Okay, listen up out there. This is Captain Han Solo speaking —

Relax, Your Splendidness. Sorry I had to grab your data recorder, but I need to set the record straight. That's right, have a seat and glare away. I just need a minute to get my point across.

First of all, I'm betting that Her Royal Pain in the Highness here probably insulted my ship. Although she sure wasn't complaining when the Falcon saved her pretty little princess hide. This baby can do point five past light speed, so you better believe I could outrun a pokey Rebel X-wing without breaking a sweat. Got it?

As for strategy, I'm just along for the ride. It's not up to me to figure out what the Imperials are thinking — I'm just here to outrun 'em.

Which I did, and didn't get any thanks for, either.

The Princess here has been jawboning me to death about the Rebellion. She says they can use every pilot they can get. Even me, she says. And just because I'm not signing on to some lost cause, she thinks I'm something less than a hero —

Leia: *What I said was that you were an unprincipled scoundrel —*

Han: *Hey, I'm talking here! Like I was saying, I never said I was a hero. I did a job, and I did it well. Now all I want is to get paid. That's fair. I have an outstanding debt, and I've got places to go. I'm ready to have a little fun in life. Ever hear of fun, Princess?*

I'm taking you all the way to the Yavin system, after all. That place is on the left side of nowhere — why do you idealists pick the worst planets to meet on, anyway?

Now, if you want to make yourself useful, stop yapping into this thing and rustle up something tasty in the galley. If you can manage to identify food products, that is. I know princesses and galleys don't mix, but maybe it's time they did.

Okay, Chewie! I'm coming! Keep your hairshirt on, will ya?

This is Captain Han Solo, signing off.

Here ya go, Your Princessness. Catch!

*　　*　　*

Now that I have my recorder back, I'll return to my account. I'd erase Captain Solo's interruption, but I think it gives you a taste of his personality. Or lack of one. You can see why he's so hard to capture in words. Crudeness like that has to be heard to be appreciated.

Han is right, though. We're all exhausted, and we do need food. And Luke is going to need his strength for the coming fight.

Maybe I *should* head for the galley. But not because Solo told me to!

I found food in the larder storage for Luke. I ate a plate myself, and found the food that Wookiees prefer. But I made sure to break into the survival ration pack for Han. I brought him a protein cube with my very own hands.

He snapped it in two with his teeth. Chewing furiously, he informed me that I was really starting to get on his nerves.

Music to my ears. I leaned over and spoke in my sweetest of tones. I told him that when he snarled like that, he sounded just like his copilot.

Chewbacca let out a long groan. I'm sure it was a laugh.

I sat with Luke while he ate. He hasn't said much. I know he's upset about Obi-Wan. The two of them formed a strong bond in a short period of time. I've left him alone, somehow knowing that's what he wanted. But there are questions I need to ask.

Luke smiled bleakly when I asked for his story. He himself hasn't quite processed how a moisture farmer from Tatooine found himself with Obi-Wan Kenobi on a mission to rescue a princess from the Death Star.

"I guess I'm starting to believe in fate," he said.

Luke related how he found Artoo, and his successful search for Ben Kenobi. He told me of the death of his aunt and uncle. How impossible it is for him to believe that Ben is really dead. His eyes were dry, his expression bleak and empty. He had just recited the facts. He didn't speak of his sadness.

But I know that kind of grief. Where there's a storm raging inside you. But you hold back the tears because you have a job to do.

Everyone I love is dead, too, I told him, thinking of Alderaan. I put my hand over his. For a moment, his fingers curled around mine and squeezed. I felt that current again. Something familiar, but vague. Like something in a dream. I took my hand away. I don't like things I don't understand. I like things to be clear.

And just then, in my head, a vision of my aunt Celly rose as clear as if she were standing in front of me. She smiled. *Patience, Leia. Illumi-*

nation comes like the sunrise. Slowly. Then all at once.

Aunt Celly was fond of riddles. She drove me nuts with them. But I can't think about how much I'll miss her. Not now.

Luke told me that his father had fought during the Clone Wars. Ben had told him that he'd been a Jedi Knight. That's where Luke got his lightsaber.

Maybe our fathers had known each other. Maybe they'd even fought together, side by side. Just like we had. But we'll never know for sure.

Luke is ready to fight. He claims to be a good pilot, and he's eager to get his hands on an X-wing. He's hoping that Han will change his mind and fight, too.

I told Luke that Solo was well-named. He wouldn't put himself on the line for a cause. But secretly, I'm hoping he will.

I know I've said harsh things about Solo. But sometimes, there's something in his face that's almost . . . noble. He did save my life. And I know he hates the Imperials. He could decide to fight.

Soon, we'll enter the orbit of Yavin. I guess I should be grateful that I'm on a smuggler's ship. Han didn't overestimate its speed. He has experience outrunning the law, so his engines are tweaked to the maximum. That has bought us precious time —

Captain Solo has just informed me that if I want a bird's-eye view of my "Base of Fools," I should scoot up to the bridge, pronto.
Base of Fools?
I was crazy to think that Solo would ever join the Rebellion.

As we hurried down the boarding ramp of the *Falcon,* the air hit us like a wet sock. The Yavin moon is a jungle planet, and the atmosphere is practically steam.

Threepio started to fret that he would rust in this climate. Artoo beeped and whistled in disagreement. But a huffy Threepio insisted that no matter what — appearance is *always* important.

I have to remember that one the next time I'm trapped in an Imperial prison cell.

Just then, an X-wing fighter zoomed overhead, then dive-bombed down toward the surface. At the last minute, it pulled out and soared to the left. The spacepilots were on maneuvers.

Luke's eyes never left the fighter. I could tell what he was thinking. He couldn't wait to get inside a cockpit.

I saw Han glance up at the X-wing, too. But he looked worried. I knew what he was thinking. Next to the Death Star, that X-wing looked awfully small.

Commander Willard hurried toward us from his speeder. He folded me into a hug that brought a lump to my throat. He had been my main Rebel contact since the early days.

He had heard about Alderaan, and he had feared the worst. He was so glad to hear I was safe.

Why did he have to mention Alderaan? The lump grew even larger, and I swallowed, forcing it down. Grief frightened me. It was so big, so total. I knew I had to feel every bit of it eventually. But not until after the battle.

So I told Willard that we had no time for sorrows. We had an attack to plan.

The countdown has begun. Artoo has been debriefed, and the Death Star plans have been analyzed. Pilots are being summoned from maneuvers, from surveillance, from rest, and ordered to suit up to attend the attack briefing.

General Dodonna is the best tactician we have. He's in charge of the strategy of the attack and will conduct the briefing. He and Willard are closeted together, studying the plans.

So it fell to me to release the supplies to Han Solo for his reward. There was no one else, and Willard asked me as a favor.

I know Han was promised a reward. But we need those supplies desperately. The metals are vital to keep tech equipment running and for possible barter in the future. Willard asked if I could get Captain Solo to forgo the reward. "Use your charm," he said. "That should melt him."

The words "fat chance" floated into my head, but I didn't say them. Solo and I had butted heads like bantha rams since we'd met. Not to mention that he's a money-grubbing scoundrel.

I couldn't tell Willard that. It was little enough to ask of me. I told him I'd do my best.

But once I was in the loading dock, watching Chewie load the supplies, I couldn't seem to find the words. Use charm on Han Solo? I might as well try to charm that tentacled creature in the Death Star trash compactor.

I expected him to bargain over the amount, but he didn't. He said it was less than he deserved — but it would do.

At that point, I would rather rip out my tongue than ask Han Solo for anything. But I'd promised Willard to try.

I'm afraid that my request came out more like a challenge. Why didn't he think of someone besides himself for a change? The Alliance needed those metals. And we'd certainly put them to better use than squandering them in some dive of a cantina.

Han shook his head. Did I think he was going to leave this booty to get blown up with the rest of us? We were all about to be space dust. Did he look like a fool?

"Do you really want me to answer that?" I said.

Han put one booted foot up on a case and leaned on his knee. His face was close to mine.

He wasn't saying that there wasn't a time to stand. But sometimes, it's better to retreat.

"You and me have seen that floating arsenal," Han said. "A bunch of X-wings are gonna be like flies buzzing around it. You know what happens to flies?"

He smashed his hand down on a box. The sound made me jump.

If I was smart, I'd hop aboard his bus and blow this planet. Stay alive to fight another day. Wouldn't it be better for my precious cause if I lived to tell the tale?

In his usual crude way, Han had laid out my choices. But he doesn't know that there's something more important than survival. Honor. I'd rather die standing than run away like a coward.

That's what I told him. But he only thought I was insulting him again. He wasn't a coward, he said. He saved my life, don't forget.

How can I forget it when he keeps reminding me?

Besides, I saved my *own* life. He *helped*.

I left him there with his precious reward. I couldn't stand to exchange another word with him. Not when all around me were pilots who were willing to die for our cause.

Luke is right. We could use Han's skills. And I still have this feeling . . . . The three of us, for a brief time, had been partners. We managed to get off the Death Star together. Our union *worked*. It felt strong.

Every time I'm with him, I feel confused. Off balance. Something about him tugs at me, makes me wonder what he's really like behind all that bluster. And something about him makes me want to give him a satisfying kick in the pants.

But I don't have time to think about what might be. I'm being signaled over the comlink. It's time for the starpilots' briefing.

LOCATION: MAIN HANGAR/MASSASSI OUTPOST

The briefing is over. Now I'm standing in the corner of the main hangar, watching the pilots ready their crafts.

Dodonna didn't lower the odds. They're slim. The Death Star has a stunning defense. It is poised for attack from a starfleet, a large-scale assault. With its massive firepower and powerful shields, it's close to invincible. Can such a massive structure be taken down by a handful of one-man fighters?

The answer is . . . maybe. Dodonna is the one who figured it out. The Death Star's size and strength is the very thing that will bring it down. Expecting armies, fleets, squadrons, the Imperials never counted on the speed, agility, and bravery of one small snub fighter.

The target area — a thermal exhaust port — is only two meters wide. The shaft leads directly to the reactor system. If the shot is on the nose, it will start a chain reaction that will destroy the Death Star.

The hangar is noisy and crowded, but organized. Everyone moves quickly and efficiently. Tanks are being fueled and weapons and droids are readied and loaded. Seeing the tiny ships makes me wince, remembering Han's comparison to buzzing insects.

But then I remember that even an insect can bring down a great beast — if the sting is accurate, and packs enough venom.

Luke's confidence makes mine surge. Han stood at the briefing with his arms crossed, a look of skepticism on his face. But Luke was smiling as he paused to talk to me afterward.

"Don't worry, Leia," he said. "Dodonna's right. It can be done. If I can bull's-eye a womp rat in a T-16, an exhaust port will be a cinch."

Luke sounds cocky to the more experienced pilots. They're glad he's joining them, but he hasn't proven himself yet. He's never even flown an X-wing before.

But I believe in him. I have that odd feeling again. I don't know *how* I know this — but I know Luke's survival is important to this battle, and to battles yet to come.

I've said a quick good-bye to Luke, wished him luck. I don't want to distract him. My thoughts are with him, and he knows it.

Artoo is being loaded onto Luke's fighter now. I've grown fond of that droid. There's something special about him, something that goes beyond programming. I'm glad he'll be with Luke.

Now the first of the fighters are taking off. The noise of the ion rockets is deafening. But I don't want to leave the hangar yet. I'll wait until the last fighter leaves.

They fly in formation, wings almost touching, light flashing on silver. They disappear into the cloud cover.

What do I feel? Hope, of course. But also plain old envy. I wish I was up there with them. I can fly a craft, but I'm no fighter pilot. I wish I had the training. But once I became a Senator, all my energy was focused in that direction.

I'll watch this battle from the war room. But next time, I'll fight.

Dodonna was just here. He looked at me keenly, as if he knew what I was thinking.

"You've fought your own battles to get here," he said. "We wouldn't have this chance if it weren't for you."

It was a kind thing to say. But I want to do more. I want to be up there, blasting away with the rest of the pilots.

He touched my arm. He told me it was time to head to the war room.

I still lingered in the hangar for a moment. Off in a corner, I spied Threepio, looking lost. He stared out to the spot where the last ship had disappeared.

"Oh, dear me," I heard him say. "Artoo, you must come back!"

The same cry was in my heart. *Luke — you must come back!*

I felt a rush of sympathy for poor Threepio. I called over to tell him that he could watch the battle with me.

He thanked me — at length. He didn't know what he'd do if he had to wait alone. I know what he means.

He deserved to be there, I told him. He'd pulled us out of some tight scrapes. But I warned him he had to be quiet. I know what a chatterbox he is.

Threepio promised he wouldn't breathe a word. Then, he hesitated. He waved one golden arm at the sky.

"A little reassurance on your part would be appreciated, Princess Leia. Do you think they can succeed?"

It doesn't matter if they *can,* I told him. They *must.*

FIFTEENTH ENTRY

LOCATION: WAR ROOM/ MASSASSI OUTPOST

I'm going to record this great battle as it's happening. Details could be important for future strategic plans. There *will* be a future.

I've stationed myself a few feet away from Dodonna, who will be the base commander to the pilots. I'll be close enough to pick up his orders with the recorder, but not close enough to distract him. The recorder should also be able to pick up the pilots' transmissions over the war room intercom.

I have a good view of the round readout screen. The X-wing fighters are blips that are now flying in formation, heading away from Yavin and its four moons.

The Death Star is heading toward *us*. The blinking light tells us where it is, and how fast it's moving. The computer will mark the time and range of the Death Star throughout the battle.

Computer: Standby alert. Death Star approaching. Estimated time to firing range, fifteen minutes.

Leia: The TIE fighters just appeared onscreen, heading for our pilots.

Dodonna: Imperial TIE fighters heading your way.

Leia: The battle has begun. My eyes keep fixing on the dot on the screen that is Luke — Red Five. I know so many of the other pilots, too — Biggs, Wedge, Porkins.

The dots assemble into a new formation as the TIE fighters approach. Heavy laser fire follows their every maneuver. TIE fighters buzz behind them.

Luke is being closely pursued by a TIE fighter. Wedge and Biggs are maneuvering to cover him.

Got him! Laser fire from Biggs just blasted the TIE into the atmosphere.

One down. But we don't have time to cheer.

Enemy fire is heavy. The pilots are dodging, climbing, barrel-rolling. But I can see that every maneuver is not only evasive action, but brings them closer to the goal — the long, narrow trench that leads to the exhaust port target. They're close enough now for the Death Star's massive laser guns to add to the fire. I can't believe how much firepower is being leveled at our forces!

Some of the Red pilots have split off to divert fire. Luke is now heading toward the surface of the Death Star, blasting as he goes.

Something is happening to his ship. He's going too fast, he can't maneuver —

Biggs: Luke, pull out! Pull out! Are you okay? Do you read? Red Five! Luke!

Leia: Answer him, Luke! Have the g forces made him black out? I can't speak. . . .

Luke: I got a little cooked, but I'm okay.

Threepio: Thank the galaxies! Oh, I'm terribly sorry, Your Highness. I won't breathe another word . . . .

Leia: The ships circle back again. Even as blinking lights on a computer screen, the ships look determined.

Porkins! We just lost him. His blip just . . . disappeared.

TIE fighters approach, turbo guns blasting. They're heading for Luke and Biggs. Hang on, Luke.

Wedge: Watch your back! Fighters above you!

Biggs: Luke, pull in!

Luke: I'm hit!

Leia: He's hit . . . Luke . . .

Luke: . . . But not bad. Artoo, see what you can do.

Leia: Threepio and I are both straining, watching the blips on the screen as if we can help them by the sheer force of our concentration.

Unidentified voice: Heavy fire zone on this side. Red Five, where are you?

Luke: I can't shake him!

Wedge: I'm on him, Luke.

Leia: Biggs and Wedge are both speeding toward Luke. But the TIE fighter is so close to Luke's ship I could swear their wings must be touching. Biggs and Wedge battle for position to flank Luke. I see the beam of laser fire from ship to ship.

Then the TIE fighter explodes. Got him!

Luke: Thanks, Wedge. That was a little too close.

Threepio: I agree wholeheartedly, Master Luke . . . oh, I'm afraid I've —

Leia: Threepio just clamped a metal hand over his mouth. If he hadn't, I would have.

Dodonna: I estimate five minutes until the Death Star is in range.

Leia: Five minutes! Not much time.

We just lost Gold Two. The blip that represents his ship brightened, then disappeared. Tiree — a good man gone.

Now Gold Leader is spinning out of control . . . .

The ship exploded. Hutch is gone. He was my friend. He piloted me once to a mission in the Belassar system. Told me jokes the whole way.

I have my eye on Gold Five. Talos Merkin is a veteran of countless campaigns. He's one of our best pilots. We can't afford to lose him.

Fire hits his wing. The ship is struggling. Its path is unsteady. It's spiraling out of control. No! Not Talos!

Computer: Death Star will be in range in three minutes.

Leia: Three minutes! Not enough time. We haven't even struck one blow!

Dodonna: Red Leader, this is Base One. Keep half your group out of range for the next run.

Leia: Red Leader is now approaching the target. He darts away, circles back, evading fire. Now he's in the trench.

He's going . . . closer . . . closer . . . almost there . . . And now the missile is away . . . .

It's a hit!

But the Death Star is still on the screen. It's just impacted on the surface. Still, it was a good solid hit. I hope it knocked Grand Moff Tarkin off his feet!

But Red Leader has lost his starboard engine. A TIE fighter is honing in on him.

I've been watching this particular blip. Unlike the other ships, it doesn't dive and circle, or practice much evasive action at all. It is relentless. And it has taken down our best pilots. Who could be piloting that fighter?

I know the answer. It's as though someone just shouted it in my ear. *It is Darth Vader himself.*

Red Leader just flared out and disappeared. Another pilot gone. The atmosphere is grim. We can count our time in seconds now.

I've started to pace.

Luke: Biggs, Wedge, we're going in full throttle.

Biggs: Luke, at that speed will you be able to pull out in time?

Luke: It'll be just like Beggar's Canyon back home.

Leia: He sounds so calm, so confident. If anyone can do it, Luke can. I believe that with my whole heart and soul as Luke dives into the trench.

Biggs and Wedge drop behind to cover his rear. Luke is at full throttle now, barreling down the trench.

Wedge is hit and has to pull out. I'm watching the blip that I know is Vader. It's honing in on Biggs. Not Biggs! No —

The X-wing just exploded. I . . . my heart hurts. I'd only just met him, but I was fond of Biggs. I remember his cocky salute to me as he climbed into the cockpit.

He was from Tatooine, too. Luke was his rival, his friend. Another loss for Luke. For all of us. We *must* win this battle!

Vader is behind him, and gaining. Not giving up. Never giving up.

A light just dimmed on Luke's fighter blip.

Dodonna: What is he . . . Luke! You switched off your targeting computer. What's wrong?

Luke: Nothing. I'm all right.

Leia: But is he? Without the computer, how will he be able to gauge distance and accuracy? I don't —

I just had the strangest sensation. It was like Luke spoke to me. *Trust me,* he said.

I do.

The TIE fighters are closing in relentlessly. Luke's ship remains steady. He's still out of range of their fire. But only by seconds.

Computer: The Death Star has cleared the planet.

We are now in range.

Leia: Hold on, Luke! But I can see the TIE fighters clustered around him. I can't believe it has come down to this. One ship against so many!

Wait — a TIE fighter just exploded! And Luke didn't fire . . .

An unfamiliar blip, moving from offscreen. I can see it now. Who is it? It's not an X-wing.

Unidentified voice: Ya-hooo!

Leia: It's Han! He came back! His bond with Luke must be greater than any of us knew. Or maybe his bond to the Rebellion?

One of the TIE wingmen just exploded. It's collided with Vader's ship! Vader is spinning out of control. He can't maneuver! Now he's off our screen, into deep space. Good riddance forever, I hope.

Han: You're all clear, kid. Now let's blow this thing and go home!

Leia: Blow it up, Luke! Send their molecules to the farthest reaches of the farthest galaxy. Do it!

The missile blinks as it approaches the target. It looks close . . .

It's a hit! Dead on! The Death Star pulsed and disappeared.

He did it! He did it! Those cheers are from everyone in the war room. And I am cheering loudest of all. I can hear Han and Luke yahooing again over the speaker like a couple of kids. I wish I were with them.

Alderaan is avenged!

The radar blips are already heading offscreen. Luke and Han are coming back to base. I have to get to the hangar. I want to be the first one to congratulate them.

If I can manage to get loose from Threepio, who has decided to give me a metallic hug.

Yes, Threepio, they did it. They did it! Ow, stop hugging me! Or at least, watch your elbows.

SIXTEENTH ENTRY

LOCATION: SENATORIAL QUARTERS/ MASSASSI OUTPOST

Willard suggested that an honor ceremony is in order, and we are all busy preparing for it. Artoo has been repaired and shined, and Threepio has asked four times for more metal polish.

It feels strange to be wearing a white gown again. I dressed this way for so long. But I've changed. I'm more a warrior than a princess now.

Han Solo has refused to participate in the ceremony. Luke tried to talk him into it, but it didn't do any good. So Luke came to me. He asked me to try. "Use your diplomatic skills," he said.

I told him that I'd rather use my blaster. But I really said it out of habit. The truth is, if I didn't think the rat would torment me, I'd give Han Solo a big, fat kiss for coming back.

I summoned Han to my chamber. As soon as he entered, he gave me a mocking bow and told me that he had come according to my "royal command."

He was trying to rile me, but I wasn't about to be baited. I had mapped out my strategy. I would stay perfectly calm. I wouldn't resort to insults and taunts.

I urged him to reconsider his decision. At great personal risk, he had returned to fight. He had acted bravely and unselfishly. And I didn't add the *for once.* See what a diplomat I can be?

It was all in a day's work, Han replied with a shrug. He blasted a few Imperial ships. No big deal. He'd done it before.

No big deal? I felt my temper rise. I pointed out acidly that he could always pawn the medal for cash.

Han didn't even bristle at my swipe. He remarked mildly that he'd rather pass on the pageantry. All that swank meant less than the rump of a womp rat, I think was his elegant phrase. Well, he would know.

I could feel irritation ticking away inside me, but I made another effort.

Okay, I said. You might be a far cry from noble. But the least you can do is recognize it when it knocks on that thick skull of yours. This is a ceremony for all of the men who fought. Not just you.

That's when he surprised me. He told me the real reason he refused to attend. The ones who deserved medals, he said, were the ones who didn't make it back.

That stopped me. I just didn't expect such a . . . generous sentiment from Han Solo. My anger left me in a rush. Now, I spoke to him as a comrade. Because even if he doesn't *want* to be, he is. No matter how he tries to wiggle out of it. So I told him what was in my heart.

The Rebellion has many heroes. But we have many battles. More men and women will die. And by honoring Han's service, and Luke's, we honor everyone who fought. It means something to the Rebel forces to have a ceremony, to stand in the throne room and see what they're fighting for. All the structures of the Republic — councils and committees and ceremonies — have been banned by the Imperials. We have to keep our traditions alive. It's part of our struggle.

"That kind of thing always gave me the willies," Han said with a shrug. "I don't belong here, sister. I'm a pirate, not a hero."

But we're all outlaws here. We're Senators without a Senate. We're renegade soldiers. Disgraced diplomats. And according to the Imperials, we're a band of traitors.

"I'm a princess without a planet, remember?" I said. "So consider yourself among friends."

Then he smiled at me in a way I usually find irritating. Somehow, I didn't mind this time. One corner of his mouth lifted, as though to smile all the way would commit him too much. He took a step toward me.

He was closer to me than I liked. "Friends?" he said. "Then shake my hand, Leia."

I gave his hand a good, firm shake. He held on. I tried to twist away, but his grip is powerful. He ran his fingers along the callouses I've developed. My hand isn't the hand of a princess anymore.

Then he had the nerve to tell me that he knew all along that I'd come around.

All my irritation surged back. I snatched back my hand. One of these days, that man is going to swagger his way right into my fist.

I dismissed him. I told him I would expect to see him at the ceremony that afternoon.

Naturally, he couldn't resist a parting shot: "For a princess without a planet, you're awful free with the orders."

I fixed him with my best regal look. "That's because I'm *so* good at giving them," I said.

I never quite feel that I've gotten the better of Han Solo. I hate that. But at least I got the last word.

LOCATION: THRONE ROOM ANNEX/MASSASSI OUTPOST

Han attended the ceremony. Until the last moment, I wasn't sure he'd show up. I masked my relief when he appeared, side by side with Luke and Chewbacca. The three of them walked toward me, down the center aisle past all our troops. It was a proud moment.

I was flanked by Willard, Dodonna, and the Rebel senators. A refurbished and shining Artoo was on the dais, along with a buffed and proud Threepio.

As I presented the medals, I felt that strange current again. This time, it ran among all of us. I got that sensation of some deep knowledge that's just beyond my grasp. Something I don't understand.

Trust it, a voice said. So I will.

I started this account thinking that it would be a useful record of Rebel strategy in case I was captured or killed. Now it appears that I'll survive — for a while, at least.

I could destroy it. After all, the Death Star has been blown to bits. But now, my reasons for keeping it have changed. I want to remember every detail — good and bad. Someday, if the Force is willing, I'll have some time to reflect.

And I want Alderaan to be remembered.

The future? Now, the strategy sessions will begin. All of our skills will come into play. Luke's abilities as a pilot will be tested again. I'll have more diplomatic missions to recruit more underground Rebel factions to join us. The more planets we can infiltrate, the stronger we will grow. Even though the destruction of the Death Star was a great victory, we all know that the Empire will strike back harshly. It won't rest, but neither will the Rebellion.

Already, Threepio has asked for some safe, diplomatic posting, as long as Artoo is along. But if Threepio craves safety, he's in the wrong universe. Until the Imperials are conquered, no one is secure.

Luke and I have the same feeling about Darth Vader — he isn't dead. We'll tangle with him again. And somehow, I suspect Han will be involved in our struggle. No matter how much he claims that he can't wait to take off.

At the banquet after the ceremony, the three of us sat together. We watched the party for a moment — everyone eating, drinking, laughing.

"Sure, everybody's happy now," Han said. "But one day, Princess, this battle with the Death Star could seem like a walk in a space park."

I hate to admit it. But I know he's right.

"I'm ready for whatever comes," Luke said.

I turned. Our eyes met. I saw a familiar determination in his gaze. My own determination. We have both lost everything we knew, everyone we loved, to the Imperials. Luke and I are very much the same.

Which means that maybe I'm not as alone as I thought.

"I'm ready, too," I said.

And may the Force be with us.